EMERY
and the
NIGHT SHADOWS

by Raquel Aleman Salas

CREATIVE ALTERNATIVES PRESS

Clovis, California

One

Meeting Her New Family

"We'll be at your new home shortly, missy." Samuel, Emery's new family member, looked at her from his rear-view mirror. She turned to gaze I out the car window at the densely forested area of her Dad's estate. Emery was trying to be strong like Grandmother Peggy always advised, but she couldn't stop the tears from trickling down her cheeks.

"I wish everything was just a nightmare," she whispered. "I miss my Mommy and Grandma Peggy."

"In a few more minutes you're going to meet your daddy, James, and your other Grandmother, Eloise." Samuel sounded cheerful, but Emery didn't feel happy. She didn't want to live with people she had never met. And she didn't want to call anybody else Grandmother, only Grandmother Peggy.

"Why can't I stay with my mommy? I can help her get better."

"We've discussed that before, missy," Samuel glanced at her through his rear view mirror. "Your mommy is in a coma and her doctor doesn't know how long or, even if, she will ever wake up."

"But I miss her," she sobbed.

"You will get to see her when her doctors fix her up. They're very good at what they do."

"Then why couldn't they fix Grandmother Peggy?" she asked.

"Your Grandma Peggy had already passed when they brought her to the hospital," Samuel replied. "I'm very sorry. I know that the two of you were very close. For your sake, I too, wish that all this was just a nightmare."

Emery looked at her feet. The mud from the cemetery grounds still clung to the sides of her shoes.

"Would you like a bag of chips?" Samuel

waved the bag in the air.

"No, thank you." Emery turned to look out the window again. She searched for people, cars, animals, any signs of life, but there weren't any.

Samuel whistled softly as he turned off the main road onto a winding dirt path and continued driving.

"Finally," Samuel announced. He parked the car, slid out, stretched, and then opened Emery's door. "You're home, missy." He reached for her, but when Emery saw the huge log house looming before her, she shrank back.

"That house is scary," she said, huddling against the seat.

"Samuel, there you are." A pretty, middle-aged woman with gray and blonde locks, came rushing out the front door. "I was wondering why you hadn't gotten in touch with us." She peeked inside the car. "There's the little princess. Oh Samuel, she's beautiful." The woman reached in and offered Emery her hand. "Come on out, baby," she urged.

Emery inched toward the door. Samuel reached into the front s eat and brought out a large envelope and handed it to the woman.

"The legal paper work didn't take as long as I thought it would, sis. Grace had everything up to date and in order. If Grace had not drawn up a will, all this would have taken months. You should be receiving more papers in the next few days. Your granddaughter is legally a Sumner now." Samuel glanced at his watch. "I better head back. I hate driving in the dark on these mountain roads."

"Thank you so much for all your legal advice," said the lady. "And thank you for taking the responsibility of driving my granddaughter home to us."

"I was just following Grace's written orders, but I'm glad I could help." He gave the woman a hug, winked at Emery, then climbed back in the car and sped away.

"Thank you, Uncle Samuel." A ruddy looking man with dark blonde curly hair hollered as he ran to them.

"I was working with my chain saw and didn't hear Uncle Samuel drive in," he said breathlessly. "That thing is louder than a chicken coop." He strode forward and smiled at Emery. Emery looked nervously at him.

"Don't be afraid, honey. I'm James, your daddy." He smiled wide, bent over and looked closely at her. "You're as beautiful as your mother, Grace," he sighed. Emery noticed that his eyes had welled with tears. He beckoned her into his open arms. Emery inched to him timidly and felt strangely comforted by his embrace.

"I'm your Grandmother, Eloise," said the lady. "Welcome to your new home. Those dark locks must be from your mommy," Eloise added.

"No, my hair looks just like Grandma Peggy's," Emery replied.

"Honey, what happened to your mommy and Grandma Peggy was horrible, and you probably feel scared and alone, but everything will be okay." Her father looked at her sympathetically.

"Your daddy and I will take care of you and we will all be praying for Grace to get healed quickly," Eloise announced.

"I want to go back to my home," Emery sobbed. "I miss my mommy and Grandma Peggy. Grandmother was always with me and now she's gone and she's never—." Emery was suddenly distracted by two very familiar sounds. "Salt ... Pepper? My dogs are here!" She sped toward the sound of their barks.

"Uncle Samuel had them shipped here before the ... ceremonies." Her father followed close at her side. "I've been working on making them homes for hours." When Emery reached the top of the slope she immediately noticed her two gray, German shepherd dogs. They were both chained to a tree.

"Salt and Pepper have always stayed inside with me." Emery threw her arms around them squeezing each of their huge necks. "I've missed you guys. I've missed you so much!"

"Supper is about done, you two," Eloise hollered from atop the hill. "Come get washed up."

"You go ahead, honey." Her father motioned for her to go to Eloise. "I better stay here and finish these dog houses or your dogs won't have a place to sleep tonight."

"Salt and Pepper have been sleeping with me since I was a baby." Emery tugged at their chains. "And they've never been chained either." She unbuckled the collars around their necks and set them free.

"Great" Her father threw his arms up and sighed. "That'll save me lots of time and hard work."

Emery sat at the dining table while Salt and Pepper played at her father's feet. She turned away and surveyed her surroundings. Her gaze continued to roam as Eloise placed food on the table. Memories of Grandmother Peggy and her home in California flashed through her mind. She wished she could make all things be like they were before the accident.

"What's going on in that pretty head of yours?" Her father came and sat beside her.

"When can I go see my mom?" she asked.

"Oh, baby." Her daddy pulled her close to him. "I promise that we'll visit her as soon as we get the okay from her doctors. For now, I want to remind you that this too, is your home."

"James." Eloise tapped him on the shoulder and handed him a book.

"Maybe you can read the little one some Bible scriptures while I finish putting the food on the table."

Emery didn't want anyone reading to her. She was too tired and too sad.

Two

Learning About God And Prayer

After supper Eloise sat in a rocking chair by the fireplace. Emery's daddy reached for a book and handed Eloise one too. What are they doing?

"Do you know any bible stories you want to share with us, honey?" he asked.

"No," she replied, her voice barely audible.

"That's okay, pumpkin, you'll learn some soon enough." Eloise gave her a beaming smile. "Tonight we're going to prove to you that your Grandmother Peggy is happy and alive in another place called Heaven."

"She's not alive. I know she's dead. I saw her being buried." Emery started to cry.

"I'm so sorry, honey." Her father embraced

her. "What your Grandmother is trying to say is that, according to this book that we call the Bible, every believer who dies here on earth goes to live in a place the Bible calls heaven. Grandma Eloise and I will teach you all about that."

"She's not my grandmother," said Emery. "I have only one grandmother and her name was Peggy. Now she's gone forever." Why did her daddy keep saying that Eloise was her grandmother?

"Grandmother Peggy is gone, but only from this earth," her daddy added. "You will get to see her again one day when you yourself get to heaven and when that time comes, you will be with her forever."

"We will all go to live in heaven one day," Eloise added. She bowed her head and began to pray. "God, we thank you for all you did for us today. I thank you for Emery. We all ask that you heal Grace and that you awaken her out of that coma quickly, and we thank you for receiving Grandmother Peggy into your heavenly home."

Her daddy leafed through the bible and began to read, First Thessalonians, chapter 4, verses 13, 14. Brothers do not be ignorant of those who die, or grieve like the rest of humanity, who have no hope. We believe that our Lord died and rose again and so we believe that God will bring with the Lord those who have died in Him. And so we will be with the Lord forever.

Emery glanced up at Eloise and studied her as she sat quietly listening to her son's every word. Eloise and Daddy have strange customs, she thought.

The crackling of the fireplace, Eloise's voice, her daddy's prayers, and the familiar snoring of her dogs reminded Emery of how tired she was. She tried to go to sleep, but her mind was tormented by flash backs of the accident. She missed her mother and Grandmother Peggy very much.

Half an hour later, Eloise closed the Bible, stood, and stretched.

"I'm ready for bed," she announced.

"I have to get up early and go enroll Emery

in home studies." Her daddy smiled at her. "At least till things settle down and we find out what's going to happen. Would you like to come with me, honey?"

"No," she replied. "I just want to go back home to my mommy."

"I'm sorry, baby. That's not possible. At least not for a while," he replied.

"But I don't want to live here. I know my mommy misses me."

"I think it's time Miss Emery went to bed," Eloise announced. "She's had a very long and tiring day."

"I'll show you to your bedroom." Her daddy reached for her hand. "I don't want to go to bed," Emery said.

"Maybe not, but your Grandma and I are very tired. Now, come on and give your grandma a goodnight kiss."

"She's not my grandma." Emery felt like crying. She didn't want to call anyone grandmother, nor did she want to replace Grandmother Peggy. She loved her too much.

"That's quite all right, Pumpkin." Eloise

inched over and embraced her. "I understand. From what my brother Samuel told me, your Grandmother Peggy was quite a lady. She was also your best friend. I won't mind if you just call me Eloise. Now try to get some sleep. Have a good night."

"Goodnight," Emery whispered. She followed her daddy up the wooden stairs into a room adjacent to a large loft. Emery noticed that a pair of her favorite pajamas had been spread on top of the bed.

"Your mom's servants packed all your favorite things and shipped
them out to us." He sat at the edge of the bed. "Honey, you're not alone."

"Daddy, why did you leave mommy and me? Why didn't you ever come see us?"

"I never left your mommy honey. She left me. Everything seemed to be okay with us, then one day I ditched work to surprise her and to spend the day with her, but she was gone."

"But you could have looked for her."

"I tried, but she left no address or phone

numbers, only a note telling me that her parents had sent her a ticket to go back to England and finish law school. I never knew she was pregnant or that they had moved to California. But, it's okay. Now you have your mommy, me, Eloise, your dogs, and you have God. God is always with you whether you see Him or not. He will help you deal with everything you are going through."

"I just want my Grandma Peggy back." Emery didn't want to hear about a god she had never heard of, she especially didn't want to hear about a god she couldn't see. Emery tried not to cry, but her eyes were already filled with tears. She turned away and faced the wall. "Can we visit my mommy?" she asked.

"Yes, as soon as she's allowed visitors. Baby, I wish with all my heart that I could take away your pain, but I can't. All I can do is pray that God takes away your pain and that He heal your mommy quickly." Her daddy kissed her on the forehead and walked softly out of the room. "I'll see you in the morning."

Emery didn't feel that her daddy was a stranger because her mommy had always talked about him and about how much they had loved each other. And now Emery understood why her daddy had never come to see her. What Emery couldn't understand was why her mommy had lied to her and told her that he had died before she was even born. Emery was also confused about her mommy's condition. What had made her go into a coma after the accident? Why couldn't she wake up? And why couldn't her doctors force her to wake up?

Half an hour later, Emery was still wide awake and still staring at the walls. She could hear her daddy's soft and consistent snoring. Emery thought that she could feel the silence of the cabin. She sat up on the bed and glanced around.

"Where's the sound of cars driving by?" she whispered. "Where's the sound of neighbors hollering, or dogs barking?" Salt and Pepper sat up, looked at her, and whined softly. Emery snuggled close to them and closed her eyes. She willed the tormenting thoughts to cease and before long, felt herself drifting off to sleep.

Three

THE SHADOWS APPEAR

Emery was reading a book in the backseat. Mom and Grandmother Peggy were chatting away as they planned the party for Emery's piano exhibition. And then, out of nowhere, a huge truck rammed against the driver seat where Grandmother Peggy was seating. The impact sent her mom crashing against the window then tumbling to the backseat. Broken glass and blood were everywhere. Emery screamed and screamed at the top of her lungs.

"Honey, it's okay. It's all right." Emery woke up cradled in her daddy's arms. "It's all right," he repeated, as he rocked her to and fro.

"It's not all right." Emery sobbed. "I don't want to have those dreams any more. I see the accident every time I go to sleep."

"I'm sorry, baby. It's a horrible thing to go through such an experience, especially when you're a child, but I promise you, the nightmares will go away soon and everything will get better."

"No, it won't because mommy won't wake up and Grandmother Peggy is gone forever."

"No one can change what happened to Mommy or your grandmother. The only thing we can do is pray that God in His mercy heals your mommy and brings her out of the coma quickly." He placed his hands on her head and began to pray. "Lord, remove every hurtful memory from my little girl's heart and spirit. Shower her with the gift of peace that only You can give."

"Will you stay with me for a while?" Emery clung to his neck.

"Of... course. Let's just hope that this twin bed will handle more than one person." He climbed next to her and rocked her in his arms. "One of these days, God will bring healing to your mind and the nightmares will stop. Even the hurtful memories will not be as painful."

Emery cried as she tossed and turned for a long time after her daddy left the room. She heard the eerie sounds of owls screeching, creatures flying past her window, and coyotes' howling pierced the darkness of the night.

"Mommy, I need you," she whispered.

Unable to go back to sleep, she slid out of bed, and tip-toed toward the edge of the loft. She glanced down into the kitchen and living room below. Eloise's and her daddy's rooms were partitioned off from the rest of the house. The light from the ceiling skylight and the brightness of the moon lighted the whole area. She could see and hear, her daddy sleeping. Maybe they're used to the weird sounds, she thought.

"Everything is dark and spooky looking," she told Salt and Pepper who stood at her side. Emery gazed toward the windows in the living room. The curtains swayed slowly

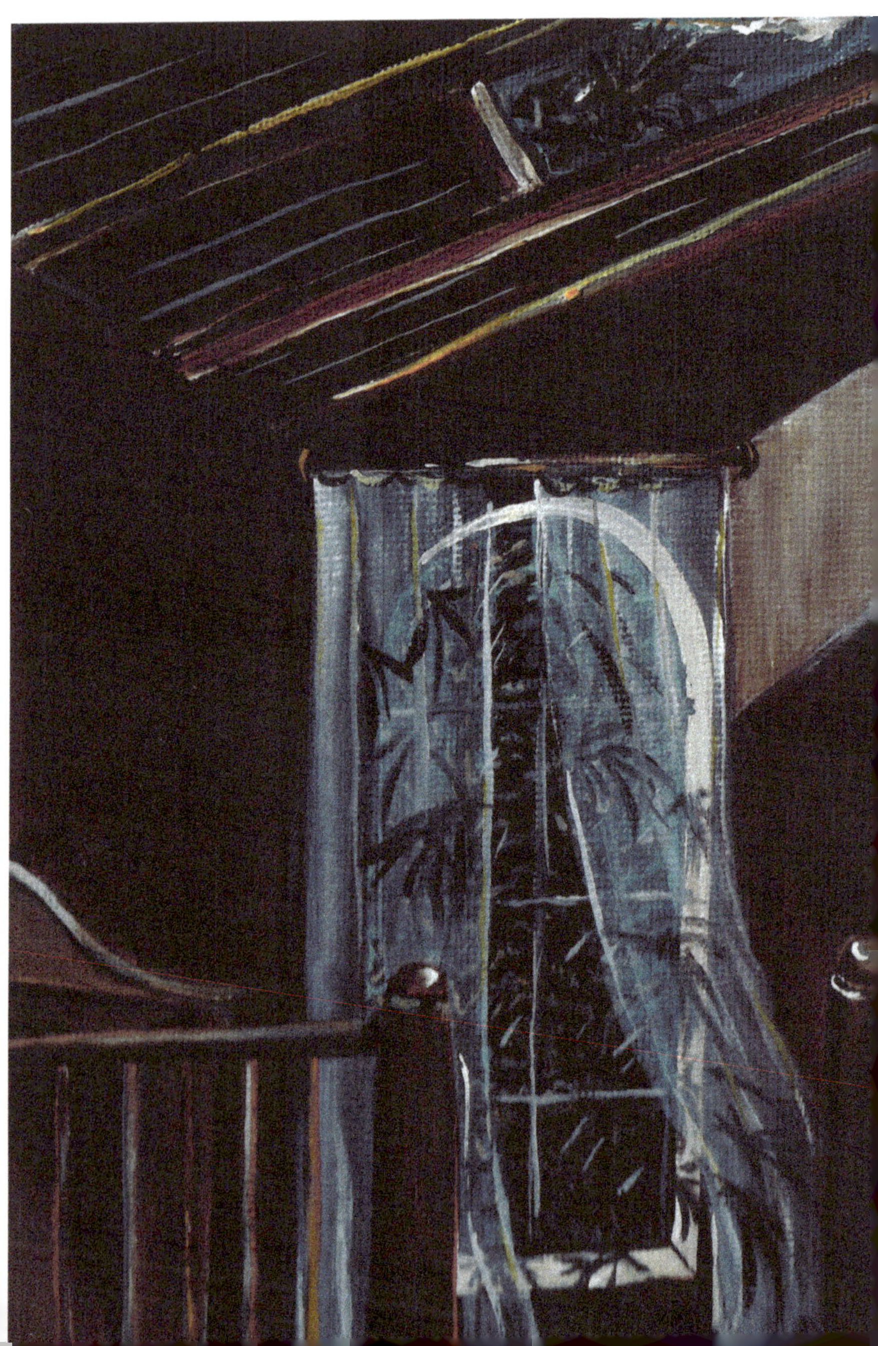

with the breeze of the night air. A glimmer of moonlight filtered through the slits in the curtains. Strange, spooky shadows seemed to sway to and fro against the dark walls. "What are those things?" She covered her mouth to keep from screaming. Her heart raced with fear as she ran back to her bed. She was about to pull the covers over her head when she noticed several giant, hairy, pointy fingers outlined on her own window curtains. They seemed to be inching closer to the opened window.

"I hate this place." She wept. She slid off the bed and scrambled underneath it, hoping the things on the windows hadn't seen her. Salt and Pepper jumped off the bed and nuzzled close to her.

Emery was terrified all through the night. She tried to tip-toe to the window a couple of times to pull it shut, but every time she came close, the horrible fingers would appear anew against the curtains.

"I have never seen such giant animals!" She nudged Salt on the head.

"Wake up guys. Why aren't you barking at the monsters?"

Emery tried to remember what Eloise had told her about praying.

"Praying simply means that you're talking to God," Eloise had said. "God ... God, I want . . ." Praying sounded odd to her ears. She shut her eyes in an effort to concentrate. "God, heal my mom and ... and..." She pressed her fists against her temples. "Why can't I pray like Eloise and my father?"

Emery dozed in and out of sleep throughout the night. Fear of the night monsters kept her from climbing back on the bed. Emery glanced at Salt and Pepper who snored loudly at her side.

"Why aren't you guys barking or growling at those things?" She nudged at them.

Four

The Night Monsters Disappear

The next morning, Emery was awakened
by the smell of bacon and the sound of
Eloise's singing. Emery crawled out from
under the bed and glanced toward her
bedroom window. The sun's rays filtered
brightly through the frilly curtains. The
monsters are gone!

"Salt? Pepper?" She looked around for
them. "They're gone! The monsters ate my
dogs!" Her heart pounded and her mind
raced as she ran toward the window and
scanned the area below. There was no sign of
them. "No, no. My dogs are dead too." Tears
streamed down her cheeks. She envisioned
them eaten and torn apart by the giant

creatures of the night. She scrambled toward the edge of the loft, overlooking the kitchen and living room.

"My dogs!" she cried. "My—" She caught sight of Salt and Pepper growling and rolling around playfully under the wooden kitchen table.

"There you are, sleepy head." Eloise smiled up at her and waved the rolling pin in her hand. "I wondered when you were going to make an appearance. Come on down, I made us some sweet biscuits."

Salt and Pepper rushed up the stairs to her.

"Good morning, sunshine." Daddy greeted her from below. "Did you sleep good last night after I prayed for you?"

"No," Emery replied. "I don't like the room. It's very scary and the monsters kept trying to get me and my dogs."

"What monsters?" Her daddy chuckled.

"There's no monsters around here, sweet cheeks." Eloise looked sympathetically at her.

"Yes, there is. I saw them!" Emery was angry that they did not believe her. "The monsters were dancing by the window and they wanted to come in and eat me and my dogs," she argued.

"Honey, I think that you dreamed about monsters because of all the stuff you have just gone through." Her daddy smiled. "Maybe you were just having another nightmare. Why don't you get washed and come down for breakfast? Your Grandma ... sorry, I meant, Eloise made us a very special breakfast."

Frustrated, Emery turned and rushed to the bathroom.

Five

LIFE IN THE COUNTRY

The first few weeks at her new home went by fast for Emery. She learned a lot about farm life. Eloise taught her how to feed all the animals on the farm. She also taught her how to care for Miss Amy, the pregnant mare and what to feed her. Emery enjoyed being around all the farm animals and she enjoyed caring for Miss Amy, but she didn't want to go anywhere near Eloise's ugly cow, Miss Lizzy. Emery was terrified of her because Miss Lizzy had big, black, bulging eyes that stared directly at her.

Eloise taught Emery how to make a yellow liquid that Eloise claimed could knock out an elephant.

"My father used this stuff on all his animals before doing surgery on them," Eloise informed her. "You need to learn how to make this stuff, baby. You never know, you might be left in charge of the farm one day."

Emery thought about what Eloise said as she watched the chickens chase each other in their cage.

"I don't think I will live here when I grow up," Emery replied, climbing atop a bale of hay.

"Why not, sweetheart?"

"Because there're too many animals and not enough people in this place and because I hate the night monsters," she replied.

"You will think differently when you grow up." Eloise laughed heartily. "Come." She motioned. "You've been watching me milk Lizzy for a while. Do you want to try? Lizzy won't hurt you, I promise."

"No, thank you, she's ugly and she scares me."

"Oh, baby." Eloise giggled. "Next to Miss Amy, Lizzy is the gentlest animal on the farm.

She won't hurt a fly."

"I still don't want to come near her."
Emery didn't believe that Miss

Lizzy was gentle. She's faking to be gentle
so she can eat me when I get near, thought
Emery.

Emery felt the coolness of the evening
breeze against her cheeks. Dark gray clouds
hovered above.

Darkness will soon be here, she thought,
willing her legs to move faster. Salt and
Pepper followed close behind. Emery feared
the hairy creatures of the night and hoped she
would be safely inside before they came out.
She glanced back at Eloise who was not far
behind.

"Hurry," Emery called. "It's getting dark."

"What're you so afraid of, baby?" Eloise
asked breathlessly and stopped to catch her
breath. "The animals in the woods are more
afraid of us then we are of them. Besides,
God is with us. God takes care of those who
believe and thrust in Him."

"Is your God going to make my mommy

wake up and get better?" "He is if it's His will. All we can do is continue praying and hope that He does."

Emery found that she was starting to believe in Eloise's God. Maybe He is real, she thought. Maybe He will decide to help Mommy wake up.

As soon as they got close to the house, Emery dashed inside and positioned herself by the living room window. She looked at the front yard suspiciously.

"No matter how many times I walk up that slope, I can't seem to get used to the height." Eloise heaved and panted as she came inside.

"Why is Daddy taking so long to get here?" Emery continued to glance out the window.

"Your daddy had a lot of things to do today, including a meeting with my brother Samuel. Maybe the meeting took longer than they expected. Why don't you go wash up? Supper will be ready shortly."

"Okay." Emery was halfway up the stairs when Eloise hollered. "Your daddy's coming,"

Eloise called. "I can see the dust from his tires over the trees and hear the roar of his truck."

Emery felt relieved. Her daddy would soon be inside the house and away from the monsters of the night.

"You better hit the shower," urged Eloise. "By the time he parks the

truck and locks the animal gates, you'll be all cleaned up?' Emery ran up the stairs.

Six

LEARNING ABOUT HEAVEN

After supper, Eloise motioned for Emery to hand her the Bible and just like they had been doing since Emery arrived, they gathered around the fireplace.

"I got all the paper work taken care of for Emery's schooling," said Daddy. "Emery's teacher, Mrs. Robinson, was very sweet and understanding. She advised that we school Emery until ..." He glanced at Emery, winked, and motioned for her to sit on his lap. "Until all the legalities get settled," he added. "Is that okay with you, honey? Do you mind if Grandma and I school you for a while?"

"She's not my grandmother," Emery whispered.

"Sony, honey." Daddy kissed her cheek. "I keep forgetting that you don't want to call her grandma."

Eloise gave her a beaming smile and reached over to give her hand a squeeze, then started to read. This time, Emery decided to pay close attention. She found that she enjoyed listening to Eloise and her daddy read.

"For God so loved the world, that He gave His only begotten son that whosoever believeth in Him shall not perish but have everlasting ljfe." Eloise's soft voice was very soothing to Emery's tormented mind. She slid off her daddy's lap and scrambled over to her two dogs, huddling between them.

What they're reading doesn't make any sense, thought Emery. Whoever God is, he wouldn't give away his only kid. And did everlasting life mean that a person could live forever? She felt very puzzled.

"If God has given us everlasting life, why is Grandma Peggy dead?" she asked.

"No one on earth knows the answer to

that question," Eloise replied. "But dying to this world means that we will be alive forever in heaven where God lives."

"And when we get to heaven, where Grandmother Peggy lives, we will see her and be alive for all eternity," her daddy added. Emery had never heard of such things before. She wanted to believe what they said so she wouldn't miss Grandmother Peggy so much, but she didn't care about having everlasting life. She just wanted Grandmother with her now.

"May I go to my room?" she asked, forcing back the tears.

"Yes, of course." Daddy placed his hands over her head as he had done before and prayed. "Lord, shower my daughter with Your love and Your presence. Give her the answers and the peace she needs." He kissed her on the head. "Have a goodnight, honey."

"Pleasant dreams, sweet cheeks." Eloise gave her a hug. "Thank you for being such a good helper today."

Emery ran up the stairs. Salt and Pepper

ran ahead. Once there, she crawled under the covers.

"I wish that what Eloise and Daddy say is true," she whispered as she

watched her dogs play. "I do believe everything they're reading, but I miss Mommy and Grandma Peggy very much."

Thinking about them always made her cry. But, living with Eloise and her daddy was not too bad, she decided. "If only I didn't have so many nightmares and if only I weren't afraid of the creatures on my windows."

Seven

Another Encounter With The Creatures of The Night

That night, in her troubled slumber, Emery heard the persistent sound of someone, or something, scratching at her window. She sat up groggily and glanced toward the sound. She gasped at the shadows outlined on her window curtains. The hairy, speechless monsters seemed to be beckoning to her.

"They're here again." Emery scrambled under the bed. Salt and Pepper followed. She trembled as she snuggled close to them. Salt and Pepper yawned repeatedly and within seconds, went back to sleep. Emery could still see the shadows swaying slowly to and fro on her bedroom floor. "Why aren't you guys barking at them?" she scolded, nudging angrily at them.

Emery tried to pray as she had heard Eloise do countless times, but realized that she was much too frightened to think straight. She thought of running down to her daddy, but felt too scared to move. Inching even closer to Salt, she covered her head and body with the sheet. "Make them go away, Lord. Make them go away," she pleaded.

Eight weeks had come and gone since Emery arrived in her new home. She spent a lot of time with Eloise and her father because they both helped with her school work. And she worked with both of them doing chores around the farm.

"Working hard keeps one's mind from wondering too much," her daddy insisted. Emery was starting to believe that was true because her nightmares had stopped and as the weeks passed, the agony of losing Grandmother Peggy became less painful.

"Come on, sweet cheeks," Eloise urged.

She handed Emery a small bucket. "Finish filling Miss Amy's oat barrel, while I clean out her stall so we can head back home. If we hurry, I will have time to bake some cookies for you and your daddy. Would you like to help?"

Emery nodded and reached for the bucket. She looked forward to helping with the farm chores. She turned and glanced at Eloise who was humming a praise song as she swept the mare's stall. Emery realized that she enjoyed being around her. Eloise is a nice lady, she thought. I like her.

"If only she would believe that the night monsters really exist," Emery whispered.

Eloise and Emery had just finished baking cookies when her daddy walked in looking dirty and exhausted.

"I finally finished repairing the chicken coop," he announced, reaching for a handful of cookies. "No wild animal will be able to get to them now. My next job is to repair Miss Amy's stall. I wouldn't want her running off into the woods with her new colt."

"I hope you can get to it before she gives birth," Eloise replied. She walked to the kitchen counter, picked up the Bible, and handed it to Daddy. "Why don't you read Miss Emery some scriptures while I set the table?"

"That's a pretty good trade off." He grinned.

Emery waited with anticipation to hear her father read by the fireplace. She found that she looked forward to that time of the day. In fact, Emery hoped Eloise too would sit down and read so she would not have to deal with the sad memories, and the hairy creatures of the dark.

"DO not hide your face from me oh Lord, do not turn your servant away in anger. Do not abandon me nor forsake me, oh God of my salvation. For though my father and my mother forsake me, the Lord will take me up."

Emery listened attentively to every word as she sat by the fireplace.

"My mommy and Grandmother abandoned me." Emery scrambled to her feet

and ran to her father, clinging tightly to him.
"My mommy and grandma promised that
they would never leave me, but they did," she
sobbed. "They both did."

"They would never willingly abandon you,
Pumpkin." Her daddy picked her up and sat
her in his lap. "They both love you so very
much."

"But Grandmother Peggy is gone forever
and mommy won't wake up."

"Your Grandmother will live in your heart
forever," he replied. "And your mommy is still
with us."

"Son, have you heard anything new on
her condition?" Eloise asked. "Uncle Samuel
called and said that Grace's attorney is
coming to town and wants to meet with us
tomorrow. Uncle Samuel suspects her lawyer
has good news."

"I know they'll have good news." Eloise
smiled. "We've all been praying very hard for
her and I believe that prayer works."

"Do you believe that too, honey?" Daddy
asked.

Emery nodded. She felt safe in his arms. She nestled close to him as Eloise took the bible and read.

Emery felt someone nudging her gently on the shoulder. She had fallen asleep in her daddy's arms.

"Wake up, sleepy head. I need to go to bed. I have to take off before sun-up if I want to make the appointment with Uncle Samuel and your mother's lawyer."

"How about the vet . . . ?" Eloise asked. "Weren't you supposed to bring him tomorrow?"

"Yes, of course. I'll go meet up with him afterward. He really needs to check Miss Amy."

"Do you think Miss Amy will be all right if you leave?' Eloise sounded concerned.

"She'll be fine," he replied, yawning. "Miss Amy doesn't seem sick, or weak. I don't think she'll have the foal for at least another two weeks. She just looks uncomfortable."

"I'm glad you had a peaceful nap in your daddy's arms." Eloise embraced her tightly.

"Are you still sleepy?"

"Even if she's not, she's just a child and a child needs rest to continue growing."

"Can I sleep with you, Daddy?" Emery clung tightly to him.

"You may, but only for tonight." Her daddy rubbed his knuckles on her head playfully. "I don't think I could ever get used to two huge dogs breathing on me while I sleep."

That night, unlike all the other nights, Emery felt safe and protected. She knew that no matter how big the monsters were, her daddy would protect her. She inched close to him and fell asleep almost instantly.

Eight

Miss Amy Gets Sick

After lunch the next day, Emery and Eloise went into the stables to check Miss Amy.

"Miss Amy doesn't look good at all," Eloise announced with a sigh. "Is she okay?"

Eloise studied the mare with a concerned expression. Emery didn't want anything bad to happen to her favorite farm animal.

"I don't understand." Eloise scratched her head as she continued to examine the mare. "She didn't look this bad yesterday. I don't like it, but it seems that Miss Amy is not going to wait another two weeks. Judging by the way she's behaving, she might not wait one more day."

"How can you tell?" Emery caressed Miss

Amy's face.

"It's something we mommies know." Eloise looked and sounded

nervous. "I pray she waits at least until your daddy gets here with the vet."

"What does she need a vet for?" Emery felt scared. "Grandmother Peggy told me that all animals had babies without doctors."

"Most animals do," answered Eloise. "But Miss Amy has problems." "What kind of problems?" Emery was suddenly anxious. She didn't want another loved one to get hurt or die.

"Well, Pumpkin, I don't know if you have ever heard about this before, but Miss Amy's foal seems to be breeched."

"What does breeched mean?" Emery stroked the mare softly. She prayed she would be okay.

"Breeched means a baby is not positioned the way a normal baby, or in Miss Amy's case, her foal should be. And because of that, she will not be able to have the foal on her own. If someone does not help her, both she and her baby will be in danger."

"Will they die?" Images of the car accident and Grandmother Peggy's funeral played immediately in her head. The memories brought tears to her eyes. "I don't want Miss Amy to die." She hugged the mare's neck tightly.

"Oh, Pumpkin, don't worry. Miss Amy will be just fine." Eloise slapped the mare on the belly playfully. "Let's pray the vet gets here in time and leave things in God's hands. Now, let's go see about giving those dogs of yours a bath. We'll come and check on Miss Amy later."

"Lord, take care of Miss Amy and her baby," Emery whispered.

Hours later, all the chores had been done and Emery's school work was finished. All that was left to do was check and make sure all the animal cages had been securely locked for the night.

Emery glanced up at the sky. The grayness had almost disappeared from the clouds and darkness was spreading slowly all across the heavens.

"The monsters will soon be here," she whispered, running ahead of Eloise. Salt and Pepper trailed at her side.

It was way past supper and there was still no sign of her daddy, or the vet. Emery could sense Eloise's apprehension, but, as always, Eloise acted as though she didn't have a care in the world. She took out her Bible and began to read aloud.

"Why is Daddy taking so long?" Emery felt anxious. She was apprehensive that he would be caught by the night monsters or that he would have an accident and go into a coma like her mom, or never come home like Grandmother Peggy.

"Your daddy will be here soon," Eloise assured her with a smile. She sounded so calm, Emery decided to trust her and stop worrying.

"The appointment with your mommy's lawyer must have taken longer than he expected. And he probably had to wait until Doctor Scot got done with whatever emergency he might have had. You have to remember that Doctor Scot is the only vet for miles and miles around. I pray that he doesn't wait till tomorrow though because the last time I checked, that mare looked really ready."

Clash! Clash!

Emery and Eloise jumped at the sudden noise. Emery ran into Eloise's arms and clung tightly to her neck.

"It's okay, sweet cheeks." Eloise giggled. "It's just Miss Amy. I have a sick feeling she's not waiting any longer. I'll go see what I can do for her till your daddy gets home. Do you want to come?"

"No." Emery trembled at the thought of being outside where the huge monsters roamed the darkness.

"It's okay. You stay here and get washed up for bed." Eloise gave her a tight squeeze before reaching for the search light by the front door. "Lock the door behind me, baby. Don't open it unless you know it's me or your daddy. I might be gone for a while." She grabbed a quilt, a huge bottle filled with the yellow fluid they had made earlier that week, and her sewing box, and then rushed out into the darkness.

Nine

NEWS ABOUT MOMMY

As soon as Eloise stepped outside, Emery
bolted the door behind her. She grabbed the
quilt on the living room sofa, climbed in
Eloise's rocking chair, and covered her face
and head. She could hear the shrill sounds
coming from Miss Amy. She must be in a
lot of pain, Emery thought. She wished she
could go help her and Eloise, but fear of the
ever-present night monsters kept her huddled
underneath the blanket. Salt and Pepper
seemed to know something was wrong
because they kept pacing up and down the
living room floor.

"Daddy . . ." Emery sobbed. "I'm scared."
She peeked from under the quilt and saw

that the hairy monsters of the night were already making their presence seen against the window curtains. "Daddy, please hurry home," she sniffled. Pepper nudged at her as if to tell her to go help Eloise.

"Get away," she cried. "You might pull the quilt off." Salt, too, pushed against Emery with her head. "You want to go out there with her, don't you?" Emery pulled tighter at the quilt.

Thump! Clash! Clank! Loud sounds echoed from the barn.

"What's happening out there? Daddy, where are you?" She peeked at the windows from under the quilt. The eerie shadows seemed to come to life with every breeze from the evening air.

Bang! Clash! Bang! The noise from the barn grew louder.

Suddenly she heard the mare's pounding hoofs as she ran past the house into the darkness of the woods. Eloise's own footsteps followed.

"Miss Amy, you better mind me and get

back in your stall," she heard Eloise holler.

"Eloise is out in the middle of all the monsters." She wiped the tears off her cheeks. Emery remembered that Eloise always prayed when she was worried. She decided to try praying. "God ... God, keep Eloise safe. Help her take care of Miss Amy, and please don't take Miss Amy to heaven."

After a while, the shrill sounds of the mare and Eloise's shouting died out in the distance. Emery could feel the eerie silence that filled the log house and wondered why the noises had stopped and what had happened to Eloise and Miss Amy. A frightening thought crept into her head as she listened anxiously for Eloise's voice.

"Oh no, no," Emery whispered. "The monsters have gotten Eloise." Salt and Pepper gave her a questioning glance. Emery thought about Eloise. She didn't want anything bad to happen to her. "I wish I could go help Eloise," she sobbed.

The ringing of the phone on the kitchen table startled her even more. "I'm not getting out of here to answer it," Emery whispered. Salt and Pepper pulled at her quilt. After several more rings, the answering machine took over.

"Mom ..., just wanted you to know that my truck broke down halfway to the farm. The vet and I hitched a ride back into town. I found a mechanic, who says he'll work on the truck right away, but I don't know how long it'll take him to fix it. By the way, I have great news. Grace's lawyer informed Uncle Samuel and me that Grace is still very weak, but wide awake and asking for me and Emery. Tell Emery that I can take her to see her mommy this weekend. I'll see you two early in the morning. Hope everything is okay."

Emery was more than happy. Her mommy was okay and was asking for her! She would get to see her in a few days. Forgetting about the eerie creatures of the night, she threw the blanket aside and twirled around the room.

"Praying does help," she giggled. "God does listen."

Ten

Confronting The Night Creatures

As suddenly as they had disappeared into the darkness, Emery heard Miss Amy and Eloise's footsteps racing abruptly past the house back toward the barn. The mare neighed loudly.

"Good girl, Miss Amy," Eloise hollered. "Keep on going. Get into your stall." Emery wanted to tell Eloise the news about her mom, but was too afraid of the monsters. Now that she didn't have to worry about her mommy, she had time to think about Eloise.

"God, Grandmother Peggy is gone forever," Emery prayed. She tried not to look at the eerie shadows dancing against the window curtains. "But those creatures are not going to take my Grandmother Eloise." Emery reached for the flashlight Eloise kept by the fireplace. "Eloise," she said with a sigh. "I will not be afraid. I believe that your God is real.

And I believe that He did not give-me a spirit of fear, but of POWER ... of POWER. Grandmother, I am coming to help you."

Emery ignored the frightful shadows as she rushed outside, flashlight in hand. She did not look to the left or to the right. She felt fearless and determined.

She had been outside for less then five minutes when the howling of the coyotes, the screeching of the owls, and the other strange noises of the wild began to echo in her ears. Fear took hold of her again.

"I can't," she cried. "I'm scared." The flashlight she carried slipped from her trembling hands and dropped to the ground. Emery sank to the ground, pressed her hands against her ears to shut out the sounds of the night, and closed her eyes tightly. She didn't

want to see any of the creatures, but she could feel their prickly and pointy fingers rubbing against her head and body. Pepper nudged at her leg and Salt pulled at her shirt, as though urging her on.

"Okay, guys." She pushed Salt and Pepper away with her eyes still closed. "I will get up and go help Grandmother. I can do this. I can." She stood and began to recite one of Eloise's Bible verses.

"God ... God ... did not give me a Spirit of fear, but of power and of love ... God," she cried. "Help my Grandmother Eloise."

Emery felt the fear begin to leave. She opened her eyes ever so slowly. Feeling around for the flash light, she grabbed it and aimed it at the monsters all around.

"What—!" Emery couldn't believe her eyes. The monsters she had been so afraid of were not monsters at all. They were pine trees, hundreds and hundreds of them. She laughed loudly. In the darkness of the night their branches had resembled long, hairy arms and their limbs looked like pointy fingers. "I can't believe I was afraid of trees." Emery could not stop giggling. She stood up, shook the dust off her pants, and ran toward the stable.

When Emery entered the stable, she found it brightly lit. Three kerosene lamps lighted the area. She was shocked at the sight. Miss Amy had obviously not waited until she got back into her stall. She was sleeping and sprawled against the wall of the barn.

"Grandmother must have given her some of the yellow liquid," Emery giggled. Miss Amy's foal was also asleep and lying on Grandmother's lap. Grandmother looked exhausted.

"Miss Amy gave me a very hard time, but it's all over." Grandmother motioned for Emery to sit by her. The skinny foal neighed softly against Grandmother's legs.

"You gave them both the yellow stuff?" Emery could not help but chuckle.

"Yes, I had no choice. Miss Amy's situation was too complicated. They'll be fine in a bit."

Emery couldn't help but smile at Grandmother's haggard appearance.

Her apron was .twisted all about her body. Her long, wavy locks looked as though she had just been in a wind storm. Her face and arms were muddy and her hands were stained with dry blood and yellow stains.

"That yellow stuff must be very powerful," Emery whispered. She turned and glanced at Miss Amy and winced at the thick, dark stitches on her belly.

"Yep, it sure is." Eloise rubbed heads with her. "I'm thankful that I listened to my heart and prepared that stuff days ago. It sure came in handy today."

"Her baby is so cute." Emery kissed the foal on the head. "Grandmother, you did a great job." Emery kissed her Grandmother on the cheek and leaned against her shoulder. "I was very worried about you. I'm so happy that you're okay. I love you, Grandmother."

"I love you more, sweet cheeks." Grandmother laughed and cried at the same time.

Eleven

GIVING GOD THANKS

Emery spent two more hours with Eloise out in the barn. The moon and the stars shone brightly above them. Emery could hear the owls hooting and the other noises coming from all the night creatures, including the howling of coyotes.

Emery was no longer afraid. And she didn't feel alone anymore. She had her daddy, her Grandmother Eloise, Salt and Pepper, and she had her Mommy. And in just a few days, she would get to see her again. Maybe she'll come and stay with us, she thought, smiling. She always told me that she still loved Daddy.

Emery reached out and held Grandmother's hand. She was grateful that she had taught her about God, heaven, and the importance of prayer. She was sure that God had healed her mom because of Grandmother Eloise's prayers. Emery looked up at the fullness of the moon, closed her eyes, and prayed.

"God, I'm very happy that You didn't take Miss Amy to heaven. I'm happy and thankful that You healed my mommy. I'm thankful that You gave me a beautiful new grandmother. I'm also thankful for the daddy You gave me and I'm grateful for my dogs. But I'm especially thankful that now I have You."

With tears streaming down her face, Grandmother leaned over and kissed Emery on the forehead. Emery smiled and snuggled closer to her Grandmother.

The End

"The prayer of a righteous man (person) is powerful and effective."

James 5:16